Emily Herman

·HUBKNUCKLES·

Pictures by
Deborah Kogan Ray

CROWN PUBLISHERS, INC.
New York

Fields Corner

Text Copyright © 1985 by Emily Herman
Illustration Copyright © 1985 by Deborah Kogan
All rights reserved. No part of this book may be reproduced
or transmitted in any form or by any means,
electronic or mechanical, including photocopying, recording,
or by any information storage and retrieval system,
without permission in writing from the publisher.
Published by Crown Publishers, Inc.,
One Park Avenue, New York, New York 10016
and simultaneously in Canada by
General Publishing Company Limited
Manufactured in the United States of America
CROWN is a trademark of Crown Publishers, Inc.

Library of Congress Cataloging in Publication data
Herman, Emily.
Hubknuckles.
Summary: Lee, certain that the Halloween ghost
that visits her family is just a trick played by
her mother or father, decides one year to go outside
and dance with Hubknuckles the ghost.
1. Children's stories, American.   [1. Halloween—Fiction.
2. Ghosts—Fiction]   I. Ray, Deborah, ill.   II. Title.
J PZ7.H43135Hu   1985   [E]   84-21355   ISBN 0-517-55646-4
10 9 8 7 6 5 4 3 2 1
First Edition

For my mother and father
—E. H.

For Raymond
—D. K. R.

Every Halloween, Hubknuckles came to our house. He'd peer in the window to catch our attention. Then he would sweep away to weave a web of mystery between the apple trees. We knew better than to go out while Hubknuckles was near. Instead, we'd watch, warm and safe, from the kitchen window, enjoying the small tickles of fear. Soon we'd go to bed and Hubknuckles would drift away. But this year was different.

"I'm not scared of Hubknuckles," I told my sisters while we decorated Halloween cookies at the kitchen table. My little brother Geoff was scraping out the inside of his jack-o'-lantern on the floor.

"You're not?" Boo exclaimed. "I am!"

"Why aren't you, Lee?" Weezy asked.

"Hubknuckles isn't real," I whispered. "Don't tell Geoff. He's too young to know, but Hubknuckles is just a sheet and a flashlight. Either Ma or Pa makes him dance."

"Maybe," said Boo, "but I wouldn't want to be the one to find out."

"Would you?" Weezy asked me.

"Sure. I'll go out tonight and dance with him."

We finished the cookies and spent the rest of the afternoon polishing apples and hanging doughnuts on strings. I could keep my mind on getting ready for trick-or-treaters while the sun was bright, but as the afternoon light faded into dusk, I began to wish I hadn't said anything about Hubknuckles. Just before supper we hurried into our costumes.

"More spaghetti, Lee?"

"No, thank you, Ma."

"You're feeling all right, aren't you?" she asked me. Spaghetti is my favorite food and usually she has to tell me when to stop eating.

"She's just excited about Halloween," Weezy said, smiling at me. Boo looked worried.

Before Ma could say anything else, the doorbell rang, interrupting our supper. Geoff raced to the door and opened it for a witch and a Superman.

They bobbed for apples, tried to catch swinging doughnuts with their teeth, and dunked for pennies in a bowl of flour. More ghosts, monsters, and cowboys arrived, and the twins came as Raggedy Ann and Andy. My face was smiling as my friends came, and as they left with wet hair or powdery noses, but my stomach was waiting.

Pa said, "We need more wood for the fire," and went out. Boo looked at me and I tried to smile back, but I was uneasy, and I wasn't surprised when a gypsy lifted her head out of the flour bowl and gasped, "What's that at the window!"

Hubknuckles was peering in, his face a glowing frown. He nodded, then drifted away and danced in the field, white robes lit faintly by the moon. I could see no feet.

But Pa wasn't in the room, so when I saw Weezy and Boo watching me, I went to the door and slipped out. Weezy said softly, "You don't have to if you don't want to."

"No, I want to," I said.

I started toward Hubknuckles, who was spinning around apple trees.

I was halfway between him and the house when he seemed to see me with his unblinking eyes and swept at me. I turned and stumbled toward the house. The air was cold. My legs were stiff. I could almost feel his long white fingers reaching for me. I looked over my shoulder to see how soon he'd catch me.

But he had stopped coming at me and was standing still. I stopped running and made a little bow. He bent low, nose almost touching the earth. He swung to the left and I to the right, and we danced.

Now he came at me again, herding me to the house, and I ran to the door, out of breath and laughing. Pa opened it for me.

PA!

"What were you doing out there?" Ma asked.

MA!

"I was dancing with Hubknuckles," I said, and started shivering. Pa hugged me and Ma brought me a cup of cocoa, and when my hands were steady enough to hold it, I took my cocoa over to the window and looked out.

Hubknuckles was staring back at me.
He swept to the right, swayed to the left,
turned and then sailed between the apple trees
and far, far away.